Gleiter, Jan
Jack London

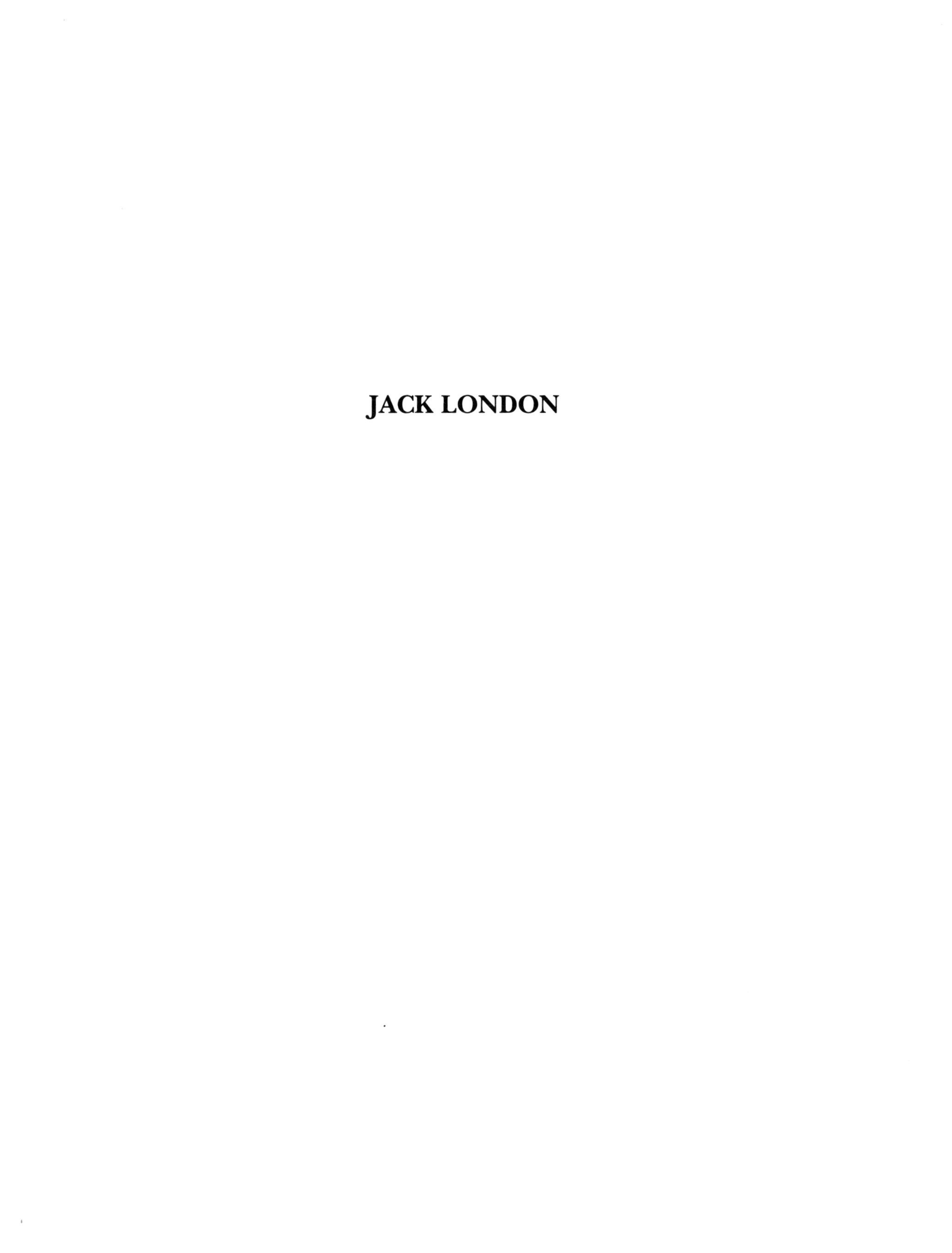

JACK LONDON

Library of Congress Number: 87-23478

1 2 3 4 5 6 7 8 9 92 91 90 89 88 87

Printed and bound in the United States of America

Library of Congress Cataloging in Publication Data

Gleiter, Jan, 1947-
Jack London.

Summary: Tells the life story of the adventurous writer who combined his experiences as a sailor and a goldminer and his love of the outdoors into many novels.

1. London, Jack, 1876-1916—Juvenile literature. 2. Authors, American—20th century—Biography—Juvenile literature. I. Thompson, Kathleen. II. Title.

PS3523.046Z633 1987 813'.52 [B] 87-23478

ISBN 0-8172-2661-3 (lib. bdg.)

ISBN 0-8172-2665-6 (softcover)

JACK LONDON

Jan Gleiter and Kathleen Thompson

Illustrated by Francis Balistreri

Raintree Childrens Books
Milwaukee

"Paper! Getchyer paper! Paper!"

Young Jack London stood on the streets of the city selling papers. It was just seven o'clock in the morning and his day stretched out long ahead of him. Next there would be school. And after school there would be more papers to sell. On Saturdays, Jack worked on an ice wagon. On Sundays, he set pins in a bowling alley.

"Paper! Getchyer paper!"

It was a lot of work for a ten-year-old boy. But his stepfather had just lost his ranch, and the family needed the money.

Some day, Jack London would be known as one of the world's greatest adventurers. When he was a boy, he was known as a bookworm. He read books at the dinner table. He read them in bed. He read them while he was walking to and from school. He even read them at recess while the other children played.

One of the most exciting days of Jack's life—and he said so many, many years later when he was famous—was the day he discovered the Oakland Public Library. The librarian, Ina Coolbrith, was also Poet Laureate of California. She guided Jack's reading for the next six years.

When Jack was thirteen, he took six dollars in pennies that he had saved from selling papers, and he bought a boat. It wasn't much of a boat, an old beat-up, half-decked skiff. But Jack added oars and a sail and painted it. Then he and his dog sailed in and out of the little coves of San Francisco Bay. He would drop his fishing line into the water and sit back with a book.

Those were the best times. But they didn't last long.

At fifteen, Jack had to leave school to go to work at the cannery. It was hard, dirty work. The smell of fish surrounded him all day. And the days were ten to twenty hours long. For this kind of work, Jack was paid ten cents an hour. Every penny of it went to support his family.

Then one day Jack heard about a boat for sale. For three hundred dollars, Jack could buy it and become a fisherman. It would be hard work, too, but he would be out in the sunshine, and he would be working for himself. The problem was in finding three hundred dollars. To Jack, it might as well have been a million.

Jack went to the person he had always gone to when he had a problem, Jenny Prentiss. When Jack was a baby, Jenny had taken care of him. When Jack's family couldn't afford to pay Jenny any more, Jenny took other jobs, but she always stayed near Jack. Her own baby had died just before Jack was born, and she thought of Jack as her own son.

Jenny Prentiss found the three hundred dollars for Jack. She gave it to him gladly, to save her boy from the cannery.

Once Jack had his new boat, his life changed. All of Jack's longing for adventure came to life when he stepped on the deck of that sloop. He was brave. He was free. He was a pirate.

Yes, he was a pirate. Jack used his new boat to become a fisherman. He used his time on the docks to become a longshoreman. But he also became a thief.

There were places in the bay where people raised oysters. They were called oyster beds, and they were privately owned. Jack and his friends used his boat to steal oysters from the beds. Later, Jack said that every friend he had from that time ended up either dead or in prison. It was a miracle, he thought, that he didn't.

But sailing a sloop in San Francisco Bay was not enough adventure for Jack London. A week before he turned seventeen, he signed on as a sailor on a sealing schooner, the *Sophia Sutherland*. The "Sophie," as Jack called her, was headed for Japan and the Bering Sea.

Jack was gone almost a year. In that year, he worked as a man among the other sailors. He learned to know the seabirds. He learned to know the sea.

When Jack got home, his mother told him about a contest in the San Francisco *Morning Call.* The newspaper was offering a prize for the best article by a young writer. Jack wrote "Story of a Typhoon Off the Coast of Japan" and sent it in to the contest. He won the twenty-five dollar prize.

The twenty-five dollars was what he would have made in two hundred and fifty hours at the cannery!

When Jack first got home, he had gone back to the cannery to work. Then he worked in a jute mill. Finally, he went to the power plant for the Oakland Street Railway and offered to work cheaply if they would teach him a trade.

The superintendent at the plant agreed. He promised that Jack would learn to be an electrician. Then he gave Jack the work of two coal shovelers who were usually paid forty dollars a month. And he paid Jack thirty. He taught Jack nothing. Luckily for Jack, an older man at the plant risked his job to tell Jack how the superintendent was cheating him. Jack left the power plant.

Jack was eighteen years old now. He had only a grade school education. He didn't have any training. And he couldn't stand the thought of spending the rest of his life in the cannery or the jute mill.

Jack became a hobo.

He hopped on freight trains and traveled across the country. He hid from the train detectives. He begged for handouts at kitchen doors. He went to Chicago and saw the World's Fair. He went to Niagara, but he never saw the falls.

He was arrested and went to jail for a month.

When Jack got out of the Erie County Penitentiary, he headed straight back home. A lot of things that he never talked about had happened to him in that one month. But he knew that he never wanted them to happen again. He wanted a different life.

At the age of nineteen, Jack entered high school as a freshman. He was a grown man among children. He was embarrassed, but he had decided that education was the only way out for him.

Jack wrote for the high school magazine. He also joined the Henry Clay Debating Society. There, the rough adventurer from the slums found other young people who loved books and talked about ideas.

In his second year, Jack decided that high school was too slow for him So he stayed home and studied on his own. Sometimes he studied for nineteen hours a day. In August of his twentieth year, he passed the entrance exams for the University of California. College was too slow for Jack, too. He stayed for only one semester. Then he went back to the studying that Ina Coolbrith had taught him how to do in the Oakland Public Library.

And he started writing. He wrote essays. He wrote short stories. He wrote poetry. Sometimes he wrote fifteen hours a day. Sometimes he forgot to eat.

But Jack was not yet a writer. For that, he had to leave home one more time.

In the year 1897, an amazing thing happened in this country. Until about 1890, the United States had always had a frontier. There was always one more piece of unexplored land, one more place a person could go to make a new life. When the frontier disappeared, the people lost a kind of dream. Gold brought it back.

Suddenly, thousands of men who had been working eighty and ninety hours a week in the factories traveled to the Yukon to search for gold and a better life. Sailors jumped ship. Farmers left their plows standing in the fields.

Jack London left his books.

It was in the Klondike that Jack London became a writer. It was here that he listened to hundreds of stories over campfires and in bars. It was here that he heard the wolves howl and saw the dogs pull sleds up the mountains. He ran the rapids, crossed glaciers, carried with him everything he would eat, wear, or use. He read Darwin's *Origin of the Species* by the light of a bacon-grease lamp.

Jack didn't find gold, but the Klondike Gold Rush made him rich, although not with money. It gave him the stories he was to write.

Within five years after he came back from the Yukon, Jack London was a famous writer. He ran for mayor of Oakland, and built himself a large ranch in the Valley of the Moon. But he never stopped trying to help the people who didn't escape from the canneries and jute mills. And he never stopped adventuring.